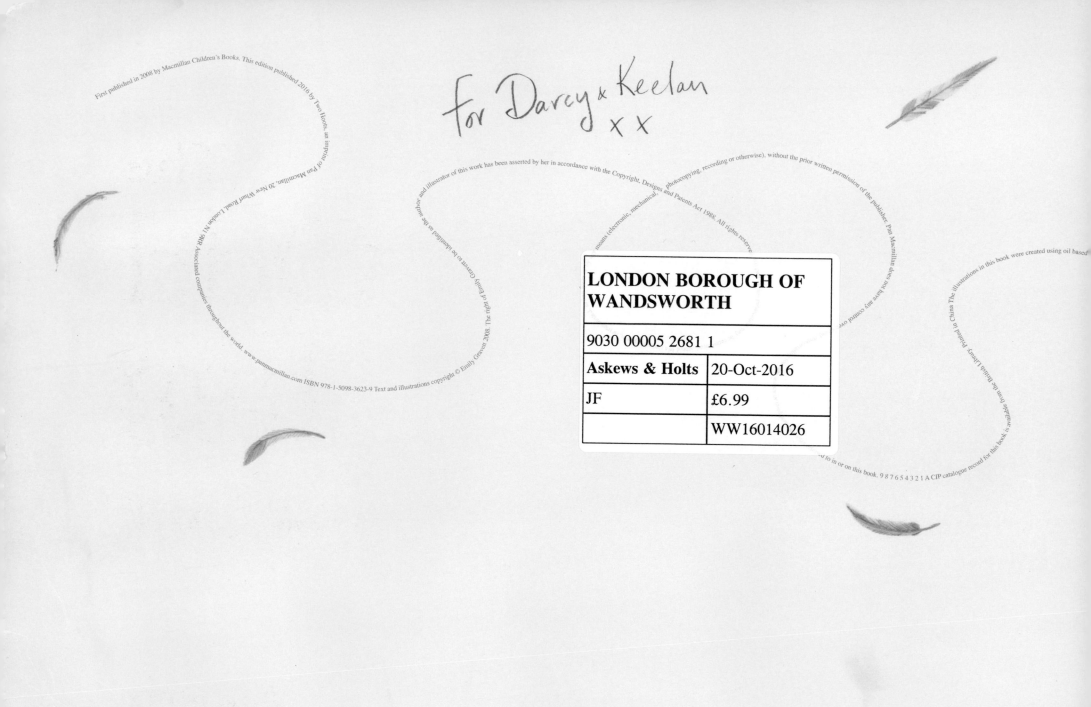

for Darcy & Keelan
x x

First published in 2008 by Macmillan Children's Books. This edition published 2016 by Two Hoots, an imprint of Pan Macmillan, 20 New Wharf Road, London N1 9RR Associated companies throughout the world. www.panmacmillan.com ISBN 978-1-5098-3623-9 Text and illustrations copyright © Emily Gravett 2008. The right of Emily Gravett to be identified as the author and illustrator of this work has been asserted by her in accordance with the Copyright, Designs and Patents Act 1988. All rights reserved. No part of this publication may be reproduced, stored in or introduced into a retrieval system, or transmitted, in any form, or by any means (electronic, mechanical, photocopying, recording or otherwise), without the prior written permission of the publisher. Pan Macmillan does not have any control over, or any responsibility for, any author or third party websites referred to in or on this book. 9 8 7 6 5 4 3 2 1 A CIP catalogue record for this book is available from the British Library. Printed in China. The illustrations in this book were created using oil based

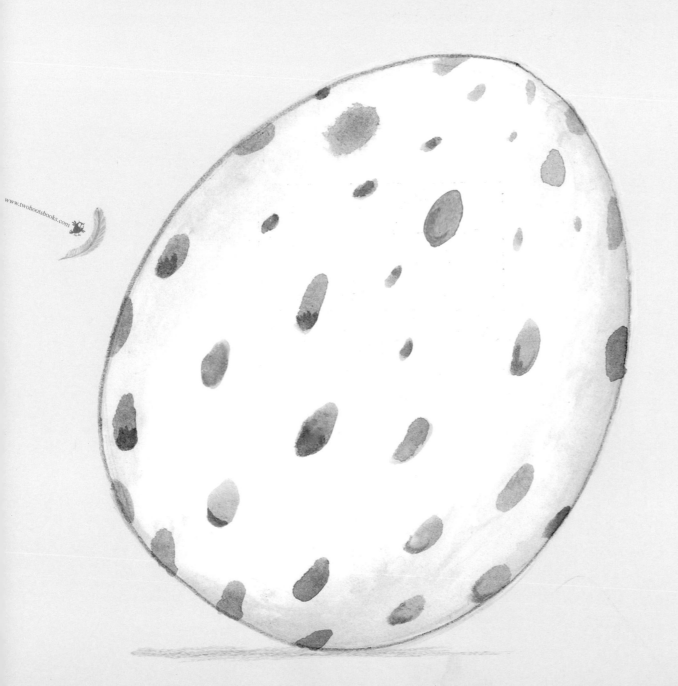

The
Odd
Egg

Emily Gravett

TW🦉 HOOTS

All the birds had laid an egg.

All except for Duck.

Then Duck found an egg!

He thought it was the most beautiful egg in the whole wide world.

But the other birds did not.

Then . . .

All the eggs had hatched.

All except for Duck's.

Duck waited for his egg to hatch.

He waited . . .

and waited . . .

and waited.

Until . . .

CREAK
CRACK